JUDAH TOURO
DIDN'T WANT TO BE FAMOUS

The author wishes to thank Ms. Adrien Gernsbacher Genet, historian of the Touro Synagogue of New Orleans, and Mr. Keith Stokes, of the 1696 Heritage Group, for generously sharing their expertise on the subject of this book.

In loving memory of Paul Joshua Friedman, 1955-2001. –A. A.

For my mom, who taught me that even the smallest deeds can make the big world a better place. –V. M.

KAR-BEN PUBLISHING, INC.
An imprint of Lerner Publishing Group, Inc.
241 First Avenue North
Minneapolis, MN 55401 USA
1-800-4-KARBEN

Website address: www.karben.com

Main body text set in Janson Text LT Std
Typeface provided by Adobe Systems

Library of Congress Cataloging-in-Publication Data

Names: Ades, Audrey, author. | Mildenberger, Vivien, illustrator.
Title: Judah Touro didn't want to be famous / Audrey Ades ; illustrated by Vivien
    Mildenberger.
Other titles: Judah Touro did not want to be famous
Description: Minneapolis, MN : Kar-Ben Publishing, [2020] | Series: Jewish heroes |
    Summary: Judah's dream of becoming a successful shopkeeper comes true but, when
    God spares his life after being wounded during the War of 1812, he begins using his
    riches to secretly help others. Includes historical and biographical note.
Identifiers: LCCN 2019007492| ISBN 9781541545618 (lb : alk. paper) |
    ISBN 9781541545625 (pb : alk. paper)
Subjects: LCSH: Touro, Judah, 1775–1854—Juvenile fiction. | CYAC: Touro, Judah,
    1775–1854—Fiction. | Philanthropists—Fiction. | Jews—United States—Fiction. |
    New Orleans (La.)—History—19th century—Fiction. | United States—History—
    War of 1812—Fiction.
Classification: LCC PZ7.1.A2398 Jud 2020 | DDC [E]—dc23

LC record available at https://lccn.loc.gov/2019007492

PJ Library Edition ISBN 978-1-72841-285-6

Manufactured in China
1-48536-49039-9/26/2019

042028.1K1/B1093/A8

JUDAH TOURO
DIDN'T WANT TO BE FAMOUS

AUDREY ADES

Illustrated by
VIVIEN MILDENBERGER

KAR-BEN
PUBLISHING

1801, the dawn of a new century.

Judah Touro's heart pounded with the beat of adventure as he looked back at Boston Harbor.

In the ship's hold were candles, soap, dried cod, rum and dozens of other goods that would fill the little shop he dreamed of opening when he docked in New Orleans.

The winds of possibility caught the sails of his ship.

Judah was on his way.

But winds can be fickle friends.

As they swept over the northern waters,
Judah's stomach tossed liked the sea.

While he was ill, thieves stole all his money.

Cold and alone, Judah looked to the heavens.

His father and grandfather had also sailed the seas.

They left their homes to practice Judaism in peace and freedom.

God had taken care of them. Judah knew God had a plan for him, too.

Five months later, Judah stood by the wood railing as his ship approached New Orleans.

Squinting toward land, he saw a swirl of brown-, black- and white-skinned people in brightly colored clothing.

Judah chuckled softly and waved back to the children along the shore.

What lifted his spirits was the sight of the busy harbor.

A busy harbor meant trade.

And trade was a business Judah knew well.

Eager to begin his new life, Judah gathered his belongings and made his way through the bustling streets.

Soon, the bell over the door at Number 27 Chartres Street was ringing all day long as townspeople stopped by to meet the newcomer and see what he had for sale.

Judah welcomed them all.

It wasn't long before he had many friends.

Judah worked hard and his business boomed.

The most successful merchant in town, Judah was happy, but he wondered . . .

His father and grandfather had been great rabbis.

Had God planned for him to be a businessman?

Judah had been in New Orleans for eleven years when the United States entered the War of 1812.

Near the end of the war, when New Orleans was attacked by the British, General Andrew Jackson put out an urgent call for soldiers.

Judah volunteered for one of the most dangerous jobs on the battlefield, bringing ammunition to soldiers.

One day, while he was carrying gunpowder to the front lines, a twelve-pound cannonball tore through his thigh.

News of Judah's injury flew through the town.

His dearest friend, Rezin Shepherd, a fellow merchant, searched for Judah through the smoke and chaos.

No one expected Judah to live through the night.

But several days later, Judah awoke in a warm bed with his friend watching over him.

Both men's eyes lit up with joy and relief.

Judah recovered at Rezin's home for a full year before he was able to walk and return to work.

While he lay in bed, he had plenty of time to think about why God had spared his life.

Before the war, Judah had focused narrowly on his business.

Now, he opened his eyes wide to the city and the people around him.

As he walked through town, he shuddered to see his homeless neighbors huddled in alleys against the winter wind.

His gut ached for the children who begged for food when they should have been in school.

And he sobbed for families torn apart by diseases like yellow fever and cholera.

Judah loved New Orleans.

He imagined a city with modern hospitals and orphanages.

He pictured safe housing, new schools and a library.

Judah looked to the heavens and smiled.

He had enough money to provide all these things.

So he did.

Judah requested only one thing in return.

He asked that his donations be kept secret.

No ceremonies . . .

No speeches . . .

No pictures in the newspaper.

Judah Touro didn't want to be famous.

But Judah didn't always get his wish.

Many of his gifts were so large that people found out about him.

One day, Judah bought a church building in the center of town and donated it to a small congregation. He believed everyone should have a place to pray.

A wealthy businessman found out that Judah was the one who had donated the building and offered him twice what Judah had paid. The businessman wanted to fill the building with shops.

Judah refused to sell.

When Judah had first arrived in New Orleans, there were very few Jews and no synagogues. But by 1840, growing trade and the arrival of many immigrants from Europe had brought nearly two thousand Jews to the city he now called home.

The name Judah means "praise," but the only thanks he ever accepted was when the rabbi invited him to open the ark when he prayed at the synagogue on Shabbat.

Judah solved many problems with his money.

But there was one big problem he could not fix.

From the time he was a boy, Judah had been taught that all people were equal in God's eyes.

Every day, African men, women and children were legally sold as slaves on the streets of New Orleans.

Quietly, Judah began to pay off their masters. He felt honored to be able to help return enslaved people to freedom.

Knowing that newly freed men had to earn a living, he taught them about trade and often gave them money to start businesses of their own.

Two weeks before he died in 1854, Judah wrote a will.

He left his money to hospitals and orphanages.

He made sure that fire departments, public parks, libraries and schools could remain open and running.

And he donated to churches and synagogues in New Orleans, throughout the United States, and around the world.

This plan made Judah happy.

Over the course of his lifetime, Judah gave away
more money than any other American of his time.

But he was not famous.

And that's just the way he wanted it.

Author's Notes

The good deeds and major events in this story are real; Judah's thoughts, feelings and the details of his day-to-day life are from the author's imagination.

Judah Touro was a quiet and private man. He didn't leave a diary. He never gave an interview to the newspapers. At the end of his life, he asked that all his personal letters be destroyed. Judah's family had taught him that helping those in need is required of all Jews. It is possible that his father, who was a rabbi at the Sephardic synagogue in Newport, Rhode Island before Judah was born, taught Judah about the Eight Levels of Giving developed by the great Jewish thinker, Maimonides. By donating in secret Judah reached the highest levels of charitable giving in Jewish tradition.

Interesting Facts About Judah Touro

Judah was born in Newport, Rhode Island, but left the town when he was very young to live first in Jamaica and then in Boston. His brother, Abraham, donated the money for the famous Touro Synagogue. Abraham, who died at 49, also bought the land for the Jewish cemetery in Newport. After his brother's death, Judah sent funds not only to support the Touro Synagogue and burial grounds in Newport, but the Newport library and schools as well.

Judah came from a family of Sephardic Jews from Spain and Portugal. His ancestors were forced to leave their countries when Jews were no longer allowed to practice their religion freely.

Judah's parents both died before his thirteenth birthday. Judah, his brother, and his sister were raised by his uncle, Isaac Hays. Hays, one of the founders of Boston's first bank, taught Judah about shipping and trade.

Although he could afford the finest clothing and the grandest mansions, Judah dressed simply and lived in a small apartment.

Judah made his fortune by selling goods in his store, but also through investments in trade, real estate and shipping.

We know about many of Judah's donations from letters that went back and forth between Judah and the people who needed money for various projects. Many of these letters were saved, and were made public after he died.

Although Judah owned many ships in his lifetime, he never sailed on any of them. He had become very seasick on his voyage to New Orleans and never stepped foot on a ship again.

The only existing photograph of Judah Touro (at right) was taken when he was 75 years old. Legend says his friends distracted him while a street photographer took the picture.